U0101171

For you, holding this

致拿着本书的你

# GMORNING, GNIGHT!

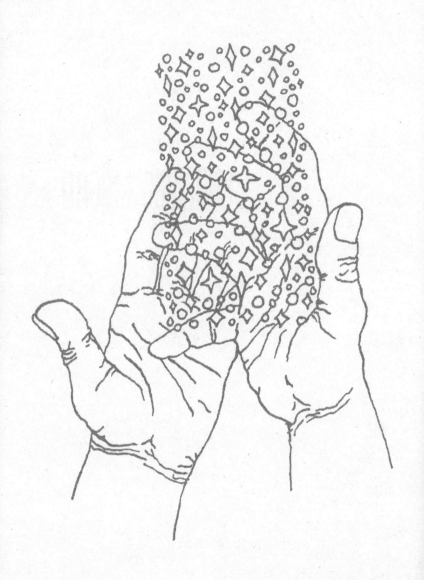

# GMORNING, GNIGHT!

# 早安，晚安！

[波多黎各] 林-曼纽尔·米兰达 (LIN-MANUEL MIRANDA) 著

[加拿大] 乔尼·孙 (JONNY SUN) 绘　符夏怡 雷亚兰 译

中国友谊出版公司

# Introduction

I wanted to wish you good morning.
I wanted to wish you good night.
I started to write these on Twitter,
A way of just being polite.

I'm really quite hooked on the Twitter,
They should take my phone out and lock it.
The biggest distraction for someone like me?
An audience up in my pocket.

So I start the day with a greeting.
And I end with a night variation.
It safeguards my evenings and weekends at home,
To sign off, a mini-vacation.

# 引 言

我想说声早上好。
我想说声晚上好。
我刚开始在推上招呼，
不过是为了礼貌。

我玩推特实在中毒，
真该有人把我手机没收锁起来。
什么最让我分心？
莫过于兜藏观众，随身携带。

于是我一早先道声好。
晚上结束时再问候一下。
我居家的夜晚和周末全靠它守卫，
等到收工，就算放个小假。

The greetings are sometimes flirtatious,
Or cheeky, or weirdly specific.
They're pulled from my life or my brain or my thoughts,
Terrific'ly Twitter prolific.

I don't have a book of quotations
Or wisdom I pull from the shelf;
Most often the greetings I wish you
Are the greetings I wish for myself.

So if I write "relax," then I'm nervous,
Or if I write, "cheer up," then I'm blue.
I'm writing what I wish somebody would say,
Then switching the pronoun to you.

And after a few years of greetings,
They started to vary in tone;
And people said, "Lin, your gmornings and nights
Are the nicest things up in my phone."

Now I get tweets like "This saved me"
Or often, "I need this reminder."
You tell me, "I printed this out and I keep it
Around, on my desk, in my binder."

有时，我的问候有些撩人，
可能放肆，或许莫名具体。
这都源自我的生活、大脑或思绪，
堪称推特刷屏王·究极体。

我不看名人名言集，
也不从书里抄些东西；
我对你送出了祝福语，
最想听这话的却常常是我自己。

若是我写下"放松"，那我其实紧张得很；
如果我写下"开心点"，心中实则全是压抑。
我写出想听别人对我说的话，
寄语对象换换，就变成了你。

招呼也打了几年，
语气自然有所改变。
有人说："林，你这早晚的寄语
是我手机里最美好的一面。"

如今推特上有人对我说："这话救了我一命。"
常常也有人评论："我正需要这句提醒。"
你们告诉我："这些话被我打印珍藏
随身携带，放在桌面，收入手记。"

So you asked, "Will you make a book, please?"
I replied, "Oh, consider it done."
Then I reached out to Kassandra Tidland
Who lit'rally RT's my best

And speaking of best T's, and besties,
There's besties I've made through my writing.
Among them is polymath Jonathan Sun,
His drawings and words so inviting.

Then we sat down together and made this;
It's the book that you hold in your hands.
You can open it at any moment or page
With the hope you find something that lands.

And it's nice to have things to hold on to,
Some kindness right here, within sight.
You can read this whenever you want to.
It will be here. Gmorning. Gnight.

你们还问:"求你了,能出本书吗?"
我回答:"噢,一定办成这事。"
于是我找了卡珊德拉·特灵
她就爱转发我最好的推特帖子。

说到帖子,还有铁子,
我不少铁子就靠写推认识。
其中乔尼·孙多才多艺,
画画和说话都挺有意思。

我们坐到一起着手工作;
做出的小书正握在你手。
你可以随时随地,随手翻阅,
希望里头有些话能说到你心头。

人生中总需要安慰支持,
一点善意,抬眼可看。
无论何时,你想读就能翻开。
它总会在。早安。晚安。

# GMORNING, GNIGHT!

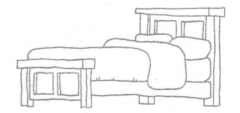

Good morning, he said.

Be at home in your head.

Make sure joy is well fed.

Don't let dread hog the bed.

早上好，他说。

我在你脑海里住得挺美。

要把快乐好好喂饱。

别让绝望"豚"在床上。

晚安吧，请休息。
今天是道考题。
你过了，过去了。
放松吧，深呼吸。

Good night now, and rest.
Today was a test.
You passed it, you're past it.
Now breathe till unstressed.

Good morning, stunner.

You're just getting started.

Your age doesn't matter.

The sun is up, the day is new.

You're just getting started.

早上好，栋梁材。

你刚踏上征途。

年岁不值一提。

煦日当空，一日崭新。

路就在前方。

Good night, stunner.

You're just getting started.

Your age doesn't matter.

The stars are out, the night is warm.

You're just getting started.


晚上好，栋梁材。

你刚踏上征途。

年岁不值一提。

繁星满天，良夜和暖。

路就在前方。

Good morning.
Good gracious.
Your smile is
contagious.


早安。
好家伙。
你的微笑
感染了我。

Good night then.
Good gracious.
You're one
for the ages.

晚安啦。
好家伙。
你这个人
真的很不错。

Good morning.
Lead with gratitude.
The air in your lungs, the sky above you.
Proceed from there.


早上好。
满怀谢意，迈步走。
冽冽晨风，朗朗晴空。
千里始于足下。

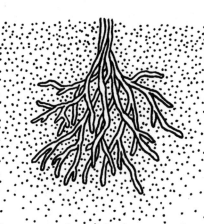

Good night.
Curl up with gratitude.
For the ground beneath you, your beating heart.
Proceed from there.


晚上好。
满怀感激，蜷起身。
身下大地，胸中热血。
高台起于垒土。

Gmorning!

You're gonna make mistakes.

You're gonna fail.

You're gonna get back up.

You're gonna break hearts.

You're gonna change minds.

You're gonna make noise.

You're gonna make music.

You're gonna be late, let's GO.


早啊！

你会犯错。

你会失败。

你会再起。

你会伤人心。

你会改人意。

你会发恶声。

你会谱乐章。

你要迟到了，快走吧。

Gnight!

You're gonna fall down.

You're gonna be tested.

You're gonna learn about yourself.

You're gonna get brave.

You're gonna take stands.

You're gonna make waves.

You're gonna make history.

You're gonna need rest, REST UP.

晚啊!

你将摔倒。

你将试炼。

你将自知。

你将获勇气。

你将取立场。

你将引领浪潮。

你将创造历史。

你得休息了，快睡吧。

Good morning!

Good morning!

Let's make some new mistakes!

Let's find the things worth saving in the mess our living makes!

早上好!

早上好!

来犯点新错误!

糟糕透顶的生活里,拣选菁华来保护!

Good night!
Good night!
Let's make some new mistakes!
Let's stumble toward success and pack some snacks for little breaks!


晚上好！
晚上好！
来犯点新错误！
跌跌撞撞闯出头，抓把零食偷闲路！

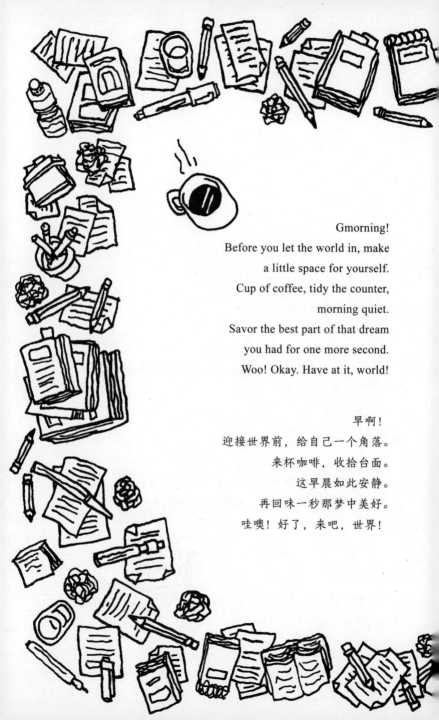

Gmorning!
Before you let the world in, make
a little space for yourself.
Cup of coffee, tidy the counter,
morning quiet.
Savor the best part of that dream
you had for one more second.
Woo! Okay. Have at it, world!


早啊!
迎接世界前,给自己一个角落。
来杯咖啡,收拾台面。
这早晨如此安静。
再回味一秒那梦中美好。
哇噢!好了,来吧,世界!

Gnight!

Before you turn the world down, make a
little space for yourself.

Brush your teeth, tidy the counter, put
down the phone.

Savor the best part of the day for one
more second.

Woo! Okay. Have at it, dreams!


晚啊!

暂别世界前,

给自己一点空间。

刷牙洗漱,收拾台面,

将手机就此放下。

回味一秒那世间快乐。

哇噢!好了,来吧,美梦!

Good morning!

Give your time, give your heart, give your talent, give someone something new.

It feels incredible.


早上好!

给予时间，给予真心，给予才华，给予某人新的东西。

感觉难以置信。

Good night!
Give your time, give your heart, give your service, give someone something you made.
It feels incredible.


晚上好！
给予时间，给予真心，给予帮助，给予某人手作之物。
感觉难以置信。

Gmorning.

Check your pockets.

Got your keys?

*waits*

Okay, let's go!


早安。

检查一下你的口袋。

钥匙带上了吗?

*等一下*

好嘞，走吧!

Gnight.

Check your brain.

Got your dreams ready?

*waits*

Okay, let's go!


晚安。

检查一下你的大脑。

美梦准备好了吗？

*等一下*

好嘞，走吧！

Gmorning.
早安。

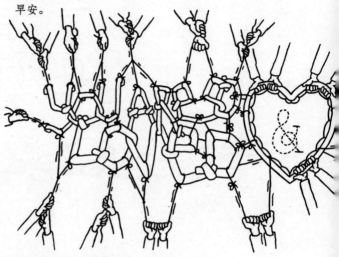

YOU ARE SO LOVED AND WE LIKE
HAVING YOU AROUND.
*ties one end of this sentence to your heart, the
other end to everyone who loves you, even the
ones you haven't heard from for a while*
*checks knots*
THERE. STAY PUT, YOU.

你好可爱，我们希望有你在身边。
*把这句话一头系在你的心上，
另外一头绑住所有爱你的人，
连好久没联系的也都算*
*看看绑好没*
好，这样就行啦。

Gnight.

晚安。

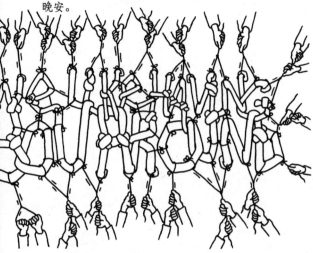

YOU ARE SO LOVED AND WE LIKE HAVING
YOU AROUND.
*ties one end of this sentence to your heart, the
other end to everyone who loves you in this life,
even if clouds obscure your view*
*checks knots*
THERE. STAY PUT, YOU.
TUG IF YOU NEED ANYTHING.

你好可爱，我们希望有你在身边。
*把这句话一头系在你心上，
另外一头绑住这辈子所有爱你的人，
即使乌云让你看不真切*
*看看绑好没*
好，这样就行啦。
有需要就扯扯绳吧。

Good morning.
Keep busy while you wait for the miracle.


早上好。
等待奇迹来临时，忙些别的。

Good night.
Get some rest while you wait for the miracle.


晚上好，
等待奇迹来临时，好好休息。

Good morning, beautiful.

Make someone happy today.

I promise you it'll bounce back.

早上好，美人儿。

今天给别人带来幸福吧。

我保证它会借力弹回。

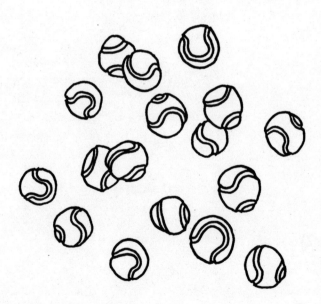

Good night, beautiful.

Make room for happiness tomorrow.

If you make room for it, it'll show up.


晚上好，美人儿。

给明天的幸福留下空间。

如果你留好空间，它就会到来。

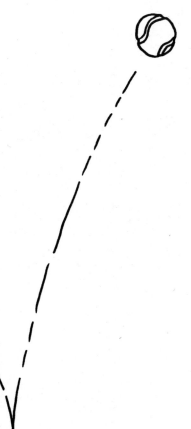

Good morning, ny, usa, world, solar system,
GALAXY, UNIVERSE, MULTIVERSE, YOU
READING THIS IN THE PALM OF YOUR HANDS.


早上好，纽约、美国、世界、太阳系，
星系、宇宙、多元宇宙，还有你——
在手掌间阅读这条信息的你。


Good night, multiverse, universe, galaxy,
solar system, world, usa, ny, YOU and your
cells, molecules, atoms, electrons, quarks.


晚上好，多元宇宙、宇宙、星系，
太阳系、世界、美国、纽约、你和你的
细胞、分子、原子、电子、夸克。

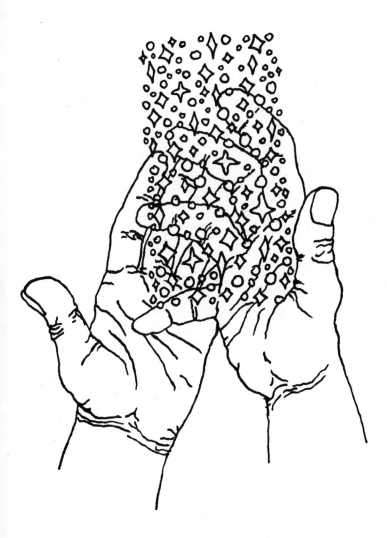

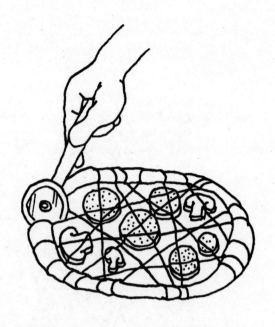

Gmorning!

Woke up achy and sad? Not alone.

Woke up with purpose and joy? Not alone.

Any way you slice it, you're not alone.

Let's go.


早啊！

一早醒来，浑身疼痛又心伤？你不是一个人。

一早醒来，踌躇满志又快乐？你不是一个人。

生活这张派，随你怎么切，你都不是一个人。

我们出发吧。

Gnight!

Headed to bed achy and sad? Not alone.

Headed to bed with gratitude and satisfaction?

Not alone.

Any way you slice it, you're not alone.

Let's zzzzzzzzzz.


晚啊！

爬上床铺，遍体鳞伤而难过？你不是一个人。

爬上床铺，满怀感激又满足？你不是一个人。

生活这张派，随你怎么切，你都不是一个人。

呼呼大睡吧。

Good morning! Face the day! If the day
looms too large, kick it in the shins so
it has to face you!


早上好！面对新一天！
如果这一天太骇人，
就给它小腿肚子来一脚
逼它面对你！


Good night. Way to face the day.
Now climb into bed with the night
and draw the shades.


晚上好。白天干得不错。
与夜晚一起爬上床
拉上窗帘吧。

Gmorning!

*quietly confident in the manifold gifts you possess,

both known and unknown to you*

Right behind you.

You got this.

早啊！

*你拥有许多自知或不自知的天赋，

令我无言信任*

做你坚实的后盾。

你没问题的。

Gnight!

*over here marveling at your manifold gifts and just
  how bright you shine, every day*

Trust your gut.

Dream big.    晚啊！

　　*你才华满满，每天夺目耀眼，
　　令我满怀惊叹*
　　相信自己的直觉。
　　大胆做梦吧。

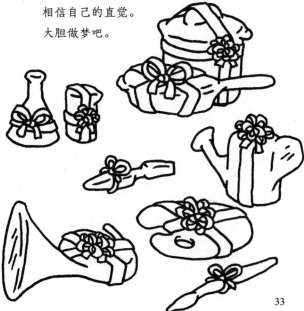

33

Gmorning!

The moment that connects you to your true passion
might be on the other side of breakfast.

Or just a baby step there.

Let's see!


早啊！

发现毕生热爱之物的那一刻
或许就在早餐后。

或许只是迈出一小步。

让我们拭目以待！

Gnight!

The moment that connects you to your true passion
might be on the other side of tonight.

Or just a baby step there.

Let's see!

晚啊！

发现毕生热爱之物的那一刻

或许就在今夜后。

或许只是迈出一小步。

让我们拭目以待！

Gmorning.

Relax your shoulders.

Gah, you didn't realize they were all tensed up,

did you?

Me neither!

Okay, let's go.


早啊。

松一松肩膀。

呀，真没想到绷成这样，

对吧？

我也一样！

好了，一起出发吧。

Gnight.

Relax those shoulders.

The day makes 'em seize up on all of us.

Oof. Get some rest.

Okay, sleep easy.


晚啊。

肩膀松松吧。

一天下来，咱们都紧绷得很。

呼。该休息了。

好了，睡个好觉吧。

Good morning, you magnificent slice of perfection.
Yeah, you.

早上好，你这块辉煌而完美的存在。
没错，说的就是你。

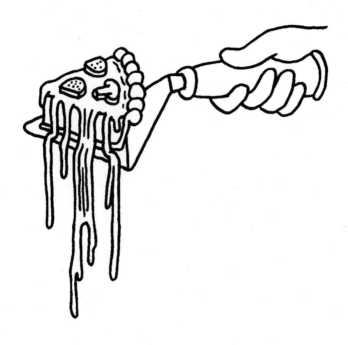

Good night, you generous helping of
flawlessness. I'M LOOKING AT YOU.

晚上好，你这满满一份的无懈可击。
我说的就是你哦。

Good morning! Wear
sensible shoes as you
kick down doors!
*Whoopshh*!


早上好！
踢开机遇之门之时，
切记穿上方便的鞋子！
哗！

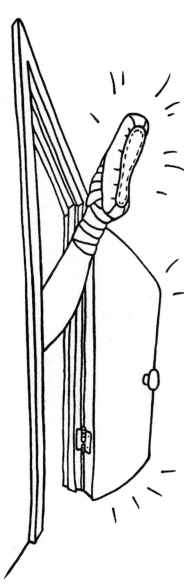

Good night! Take off your sensible shoes, put on your dancin' shoes, you deserve it.

晚上好！
脱下方便的鞋子，
换上舞鞋吧，
是你应得的。

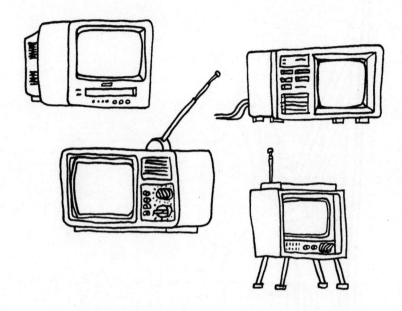

Good morning.

Everything could change today.

Or one tiny, vital thing.

What it WON'T be is a rerun of yesterday.

Let's see.


早上好。

今日一切都可能改变。

又或只是微小而关键的一件事。

它不可能是昨日重映。

拭目以待吧。

Good night.

Everything could change tomorrow.

Or one tiny, vital thing.

What it WON'T be is a rerun of today.

Rest up.


晚上好。

明日一切都可能改变。

又或只是微小而关键的一件事。

它不可能是今日重映。

好好休息吧。

Gmorning, love.
Your best impulse, that selfless impulse, let
it take the wheel.
Let it drive you toward the person you
dreamed you'd be.

早安，亲爱的。
让你那份最好的直觉——
无私的直觉掌控方向盘。
让它带你驶向你梦想成为的人。

Gnight, love.

That need to rest, that constructive impulse, let
it take the lead.

I hope you dream the best, coolest shit. Let's go.


晚安，亲爱的。

让那份休息的需求，

那份建设性的直觉带领你。

愿你好梦，梦见最好最酷的玩意。赶快睡吧。

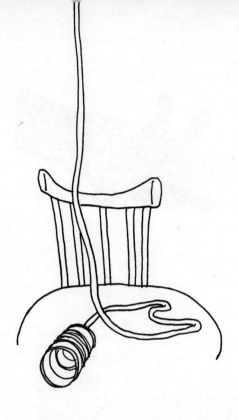

Call that friend you keep meaning to call, despite
the time that's piled up. Pride is dumb. They miss you
too. Good morning!

打电话给那位你一直想联系的友人吧，无论时间堆积多少。
骄傲不值一提。对方也想念着你。早上好！

Good night. Hope you called that friend of yours!

晚上好，希望你给那位朋友打电话了！

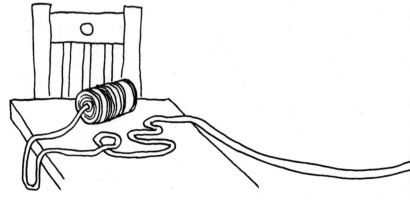

Gmorning.

Breathe deep.

That hitch in your breath is a record scratch.

That throbbing in your temple is the bass, and you
control the volume knob.

The scars in your mind and your heart are grooves
that run deep. YOUR music. YOUR heart. YOUR life.

You got the aux cord.

Bump it.


早啊。

深呼吸。

呼吸里那一次卡顿是磁带上的刮伤。

太阳穴的胀痛是低音轰鸣，你手中正捏着音量旋钮。

你脑海里和心头上的伤痕是音乐里的动感韵味

深深缠绕于旋律之中。

这是你的音乐。你的心灵。你的生活。

音频线正握在你手。

躁起来。

Gnight.

You got the aux cord.

Your mind is your own.

Your heart is your own.

You set the playlist.

Bump it.


晚啊。

音频线就在你手中。

你的思想属于自己。

你的心灵属于自己。

播放列表是你说了算。

躁起来。

Good morning!
When you were born you held infinite promise.
You're older, you're all banged up by life,
But you hold that promise still.


早上好！
诞生于世那一刻，你拥有无限希望。
年岁渐长，生活令你遍体鳞伤，
但那希望仍在你手。

Good night!

When you were born you held infinite promise.

You're older, you're all banged up by life,

But you hold that promise still.

KEEP GOING.

晚上好！

诞生于世那一刻，你拥有无限希望。

年岁渐长，生活令你遍体鳞伤，

但那希望仍在你手。

坚持下去。

GMORNING.

Grateful for the very NOTION of you, even more grateful for the reality.

Look at you, a dream realized.

We're off! Let's go!

早啊。

感谢有你，更感谢
你真的存在。

看啊，你是成真的美梦。

出发了！走吧！

GNIGHT.

Grateful for the REALITY of you, even more grateful for the notion of tomorrow.

Rest up. We need you at your best.


晚啊。

感谢你真的存在，更加感谢
还有明天。

休息吧。我们需要你状态完美。

Good morning.
Sometimes staying under the covers
seems like the best option.
I feel you.
But cmon, let's go see
what's out there.

早安。
有时，赖在被窝里仿佛是
最好的选择。
我懂你。
但振作点，一起来
看看外头的世界吧。

And there is your comfy bed,
right where you left it.
You earned this good rest.
Good night.

这舒适的床铺
还在原处等你。
这是你应得的休憩。
晚安。

Good morning, you Matryoshka dolls,
you carry so many versions of yourself
around inside you.
Take a seat, chill for a minute.


早上好呀，你这俄罗斯套娃，
你将这么多层不一样的自己
包裹着藏于内心。
坐下来，休息片刻吧。

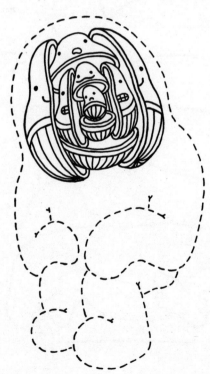

Good night, you Matryoshka dolls,
stack 'em up and pack 'em in.
You contain multitudes.


晚安，你这俄罗斯套娃，
把娃娃都堆起来，收拾好。
你有无限潜力。

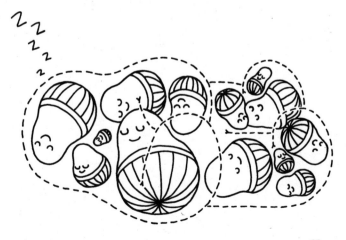

Good morning.
Take a breath.
Then another.
Repeat.
Move at your pace.
You got this.


早上好。
吸气。
吐气。重复。
你主宰自己的节奏。
你能行。

Good night.
Take a breath.
Then another.
Repeat.
Shake off the day.
Sweet dreams.

晚上好。
吸气。
吐气。重复。
甩掉一天的疲惫。
做个好梦。

Gmorning, friendos!
Make good choices!
Listen to your
inside voices!

早安，伙伴们！
抉择时保持机敏！
倾听你们
内心的声音！

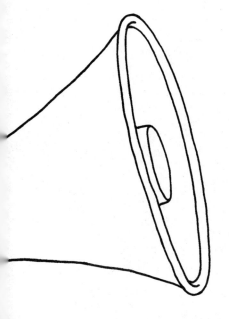

Gnight, friendos!
Make good choices!
Live your life
and raise your voices!

晚安，伙伴们！
抉择时保持机敏！
过好生活，
大声发出自己的声音！

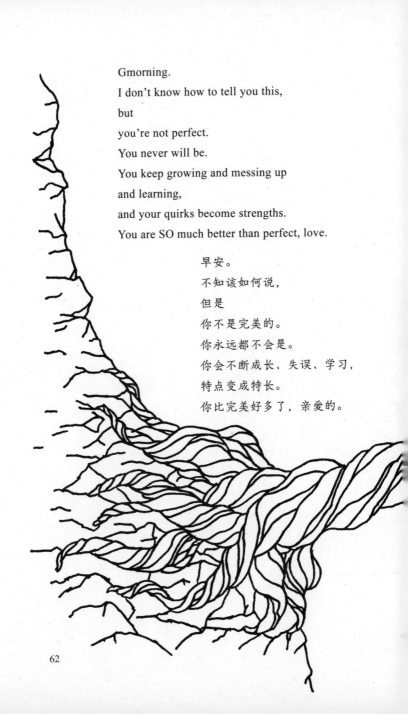

Gmorning.

I don't know how to tell you this,

but

you're not perfect.

You never will be.

You keep growing and messing up

and learning,

and your quirks become strengths.

You are SO much better than perfect, love.

早安。

不知该如何说，

但是

你不是完美的。

你永远都不会是。

你会不断成长、失误、学习，

特点变成特长。

你比完美好多了，亲爱的。

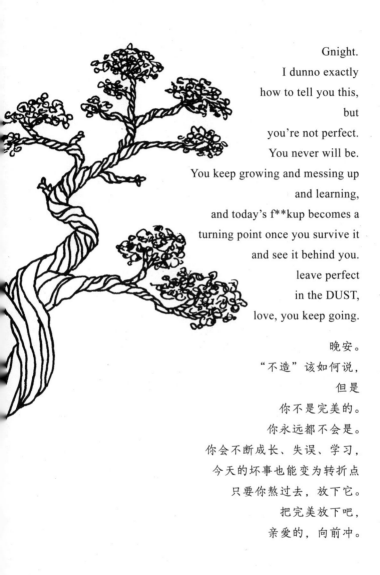

Gnight.
I dunno exactly
how to tell you this,
but
you're not perfect.
You never will be.
You keep growing and messing up
and learning,
and today's f**kup becomes a
turning point once you survive it
and see it behind you.
leave perfect
in the DUST,
love, you keep going.

晚安。
"不造"该如何说，
但是
你不是完美的。
你永远都不会是。
你会不断成长、失误、学习，
今天的坏事也能变为转折点
只要你熬过去，放下它。
把完美放下吧，
亲爱的，向前冲。

63

Gmorning.

Crawl before you walk before you run before you fly

before you ASCEND TO GREATNESS

& get some food in you, maybe a banana.

*Vamos*!

早安。

学会爬再走，学会走再跑，学会跑再飞，

学会飞再羽化登仙

记得吃点东西，也许吃根香蕉。

走咯！

Gnight.

Brush your teeth before you sleep before you dream before
you fly before you CHANGE THE WORLD.

And stay hydrated!

晚安。

刷了牙再睡觉，睡着了再入梦，

入梦了再飞起，飞起来再改变世界。

记得喝水！

Good morning.

You've been playing this open-world game for a while now.

Complete a mission today.

Gain some new powers.

早上好。

你玩这个开放世界式游戏有段时间了。

完成今日任务。

掌握新的能力。

Good night, kids.
Level up.

晚上好，孩子们。
通关了哦。

Good morning, you.

It's been a minute.

*smiles*

MY FRIEND LIKES YOU.

*runs away*

早上好呀，说的就是你。

有一阵子不见了。

*露出微笑*

我有个朋友喜欢你。

*转身跑开*

Good night, you.

It's been a minute.

*walks away, shouts over shoulder*

THE FRIEND WAS ME, I'M THE FRIEND.

*runs out of sight*


晚上好呀，说的就是你。

有一阵子不见了。

*转身走开，回头大喊*

那朋友是我，我就是那个朋友。

*跑出你的视线*

Gmorning!
I wish you clarity today.
Clarity of thought, clarity of expression, and a direct
line between what you feel and what to do about it.


早啊！
愿你今天清清爽爽。
思绪清爽，谈吐清爽，直截了当地
看清自己所思所想，坦然应对。

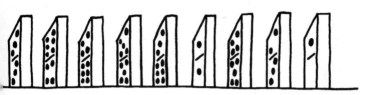

Gnight!

I wish you clarity tonight.

Clarity of self, clarity of purpose, and a direct line between
who you want to be and how to get there.


晚啊!

愿你今晚明明白白。

明白自己，明白目标，明确地
知晓理想中自己的模样，坚定去追。

Things may never be like this again.
That could be good news or bad news to
you, but it's true nonetheless.
Gmorning.


今日一切或许不再。
未来对你或许有好有坏，
但无论如何，世事如此。
早啊。


Everything is changing all the time.
May as well lean into it.
Gnight!


万事万物永远无定。
不如倾情投入。
晚啊！

Good morning!
Get after what you want.
Leave excuses on the side of the road.
Don't you feel lighter?


早上好!
追求你的渴望。
将犹疑抛在路边。
不觉得一身轻松吗?

Good night.

We're closer than where we started.

Nothing but open road ahead.

Let's go!

晚上好。

我们已经比开始更进一步。

面前只有大路朝天。

出发吧!

Gmorning!

Write a bit, just for yourself.

Give that maelstrom in your head a place to land.

Look at everything swirling around in there!

早啊!

写点什么吧,就为了你自己。

给你脑中那团混沌无明寻处落脚。

看看你脑子里乱哄哄地转着多少繁杂!

Write some thoughts down for yourself.

Grab what you can, pin it to the page.

Look at that! How long you been hanging on to those?

Gnight!


为自己落笔写点什么吧。

抓住思绪，落于纸端。

看看！这些东西你都记挂多久了？

晚啊！

Peep the pep in your step
and the glide in your stride.
You're a knockout, my friend.
Let yourself be your guide.
Gmorning!

蹦蹦跳跳办事去，
大步流星闯出来。
你真是牛，朋友。
就来引领自己的精彩。
早啊！

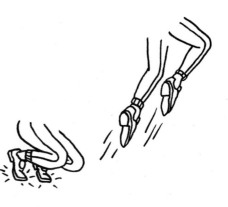

Jaws will drop as you bop,

catch your eye passing by.

You're a knockout, my friend.

Be yourself, let it fly.

Gnight!


潇洒而过，留下满地惊叹；

飘然行来，你是众人焦点。

你真的牛，朋友。

坚持真我，一飞冲天。

晚安！

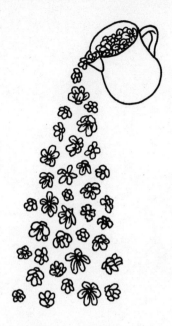

Gmorning.

You've got stuff in your head that no one else has got.

And you've got stuff in your head that you think you

bear alone, but I PROMISE you share with so many.

Only way to know the difference is to spill it out.

On paper, into a mic, to a shrink, onto a canvas.

Let's go!


早啊。

你有些思想在这世上独一无二。

还有些想法你自以为

独一无二，但我保证不少人也这样想。

想知道究竟如何，只能把它表达出来。

放在纸上，说给话筒，告诉医生，落于画布。

来吧！

Gnight.

Rest your gifts,

rest your burdens,

rest your secrets,

rest your dreams,

rest your unrequited loves, rest the loves that

sustain you.

Tomorrow you can harvest them all again.

On paper, into a mic, to a shrink, onto a canvas.

For now, rest.


晚啊。

放下你的才能，

放下你的负担，

放下你的秘密，

放下你的梦想，

放下你无人回应的爱，

放下那支持着你的种种爱意。

明天你就能把它们再一次收获。

来自纸上，来自话筒，来自医生，来自画布。

现在，休息吧。

You're so pretty I can't look directly at you.
You're an eclipse.
Good morning.


你的美丽令我无法直视。
你吞食了太阳的光辉。
早上好。

The sun is gone but you remain,
undimmed and glorious.
Good night.

日已西沉，但你仍在，
光明如一，辉煌如一。
晚上好。

# HAVE A GOOD MORNING NO PRESSURE
# THOUGH

过个好早晨
不过别有压力呀

HAVE A GOOD NIGHT EVERYONE IS
COUNTING ON YOU
SWEET DREAMS

晚上好好过
大家全都
指望着你呢
好梦

Good morning.

I'm tired. I bet you're tired.

But we're awake and alive and that's enough. Cmon.

Cmon.


早上好。

我累了，我打赌你也是。

但我们醒了，活着，就够了。振作点。

振作点。

Good night.

I'm tired. I bet you're tired.

But we're awake and alive and that's enough. Cmon.

Cmon.

晚上好。

我累了，我打赌你也是。

但我们还醒着，还活着，就够了。振作点。

振作点。

Gmorning.

Inertia's a helluva drug.

If you've been going nonstop,

be an object at rest.

If you've been at rest too long,

get in motion.

Don't rely on an external force,

kick inertia in the grundle, let's GO.


早啊。

惯性的劲头真大。

如果你一直忙忙碌碌，

就静止下来吧。

如果你休息得太久，

就动起来吧。

别指望外力推你一把，

狠狠踢惯性一脚，赶紧行动起来。

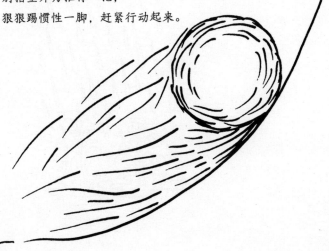

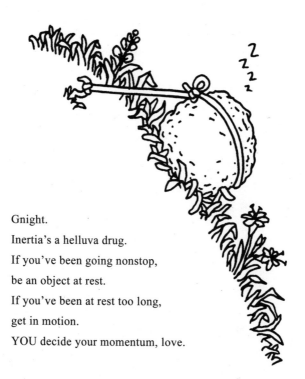

Gnight.

Inertia's a helluva drug.

If you've been going nonstop,

be an object at rest.

If you've been at rest too long,

get in motion.

YOU decide your momentum, love.


晚啊。

惯性的劲头真大。

如果你一直忙忙碌碌，

就静止下来吧。

如果你休息得太久，

就动起来吧。

你才能决定自己的动向，亲爱的。

Gmorning!

Your mind is yours alone.

Do what it takes to make yourself comfy.

Build a library in there, play some music.

Make it your home.

早安！

你的思想唯你独有。

去做任何事，只需让你舒适。

在脑海建造图书馆，播放音乐。

让它成为你的家。

Gnight!

Your mind is yours alone.

Do what it takes to make yourself comfy.

Draw the blinds, kick out unwelcome guests.

Make it your home.


晚安！

你的思想唯你独有。

去做任何事，只需让你舒适。

拉上窗帘，赶走不速之客。

让它成为你的家。

Good morning!
*engages in complicated
  handshake that injures us both*
Ow! Worth it! Go get'em!


早上好!
*进行一番复杂的握手,
  我们俩都受了伤*
啊! 但是值得! 动手吧!

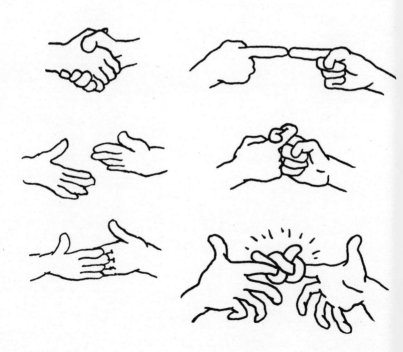

Good night!

*engages in complicated handshake that
  injures us both*

Oops! Put ice on that! Get some rest!


晚上好!

*进行一番复杂的握手,
  我们俩都受了伤*

哎呀不好意思! 冰敷一下吧! 好好休息!

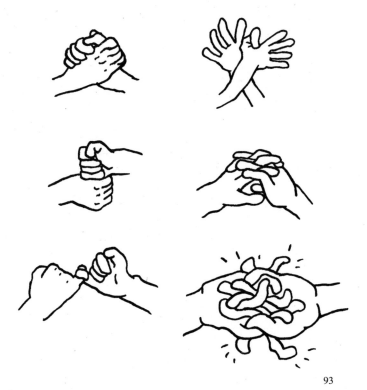

Gmorning.

In your corner,

even in the roundest of rooms.

On your side,

even if it makes this seesaw kind of boring.


早安。

在角落为你摇旗呐喊，

即使在最圆的房间。

在你身边，

即使它让这个跷跷板有些无聊。

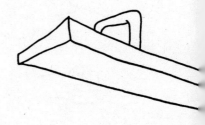

Gnight.

Holding your hand,

even if it's sticky from jelly or honey.

On your team,

even when you're playing solitaire.

晚安，

拉住你的手，

即使上面粘着黏黏的果酱或是蜂蜜。

和你是一队，

即使你在玩单人纸牌。

The world changes.
The ground shifts.
We still make plans.
We still find gifts.
Gmorning.


世界变化。
沧海桑田。
未来仍在规划。
馈赠仍需找寻。
早安。

The world changes.
The earth spins.
We grieve our losses.
We eke out wins.
Gnight.

世界变化。
地球不息。
我们哀悼失去。
我们拼搏胜利。
晚安。

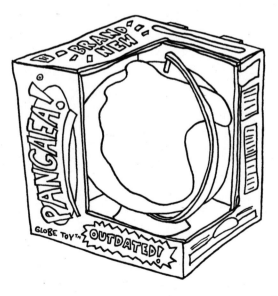

Good morning.

Put some music in someone else's life today.

Make the world a mixtape and see what it gives
you in return.

早上好。

今天为别人的生活放点音乐吧。

给世界做一盘混音带，

看看它会给出什么回赠。

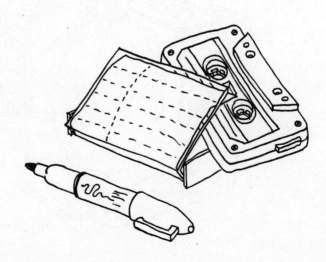

Good night.
Put some music in your life tonight.
Make yourself a mixtape and see where
your heart goes.


晚上好。
今晚为自己的生活放点音乐吧。
给自己做一盘混音带，
看看你的心会走向何方。

*stands at roulette table*

Gmorning!

*pushes all the chips in your direction*

I'm betting on YOU.

Dealer: Sir, that's not how this works—


*站在俄罗斯轮盘赌桌前*

早安！

*把所有的筹码推向你的方向*

我赌在你身上。

荷官：先生，不是这么玩的——

*stands at the craps table*

Gnight!

*rolls dice*

I'm rolling the dice on YOU.

*begins singing "Luck Be a Lady"*

Dealer: Sir, are you playing or—


*站在骰子赌桌前*

晚安！

*掷骰*

我赌骰子押注是你。

*唱起《幸运是一位淑女》*

荷官：先生，您到底玩不玩——

Good morning.

Your pace today.

No one else's.

You can't be rushed, you can't be slowed down.


早上好，

今天由你的节奏定义。

而不是其他任何人。

你不能被催促前进，你不能被拖慢脚步。

Good night.

Your pace in this life.

No one else's.

You can't be rushed, you can't be slowed down.


晚上好，

此生由你的节奏定义。

而不是其他任何人。

你不能被催促前进，你不能被拖慢脚步。

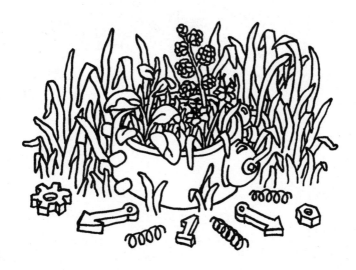

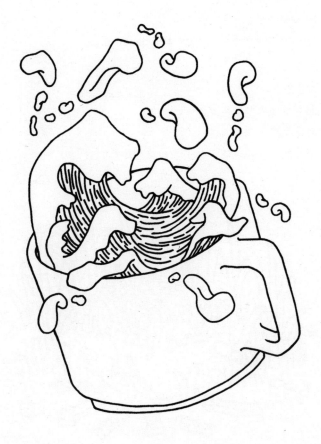

Good morning.
Woke up grateful for the air
in my lungs, the sleep in my eyes,
the ache in my bones,
the chance to say hello again.


早上好。
醒来之时，
感恩空气充满我的肺叶，
睡意留在我的眼睛，
酸痛萦绕我的骨头，
有机会能再说你好。


Good night.
Lying down grateful for the air
in my lungs, the sleep in my eyes,
the ache in my bones,
the chance to see you tomorrow.


晚上好。
躺下之时，
感恩空气充满我的肺叶，
睡意留在我的眼睛，
酸痛萦绕我的骨头，
有机会明天再见你。

Gmorning.

Untie just ONE of the knots in your stomach.

Cross ONE thing off your list.

Call ONE loved one and surprise them with some kindness.

Damn, look at all the ROOM YOU MADE FOR SOMETHING NEW, KID.


早安。

只解开一个心里的结。

只划掉一件要做的事。

给一位亲友打电话，以善意给他们惊喜。

天哪，看看你为新事物造出的那么多空间，孩子。

Gnight.

There are still knots in your stomach.

Mine too.

A good night's rest won't undo them completely, but it loosens their grip and softens the strands.

Close your eyes and

MAKE ROOM FOR SOMETHING NEW, KID.

晚安。

你心里仍然有结。

我也有。

好好休息一晚上，虽然无法完全解开它们，

但是能让它们得到松缓。

闭上眼睛，

为新事物制造出空间，孩子。

Good morning.
You are stunning.
Use your power wisely.


早上好。
你魅力四射。
慎用你的力量。

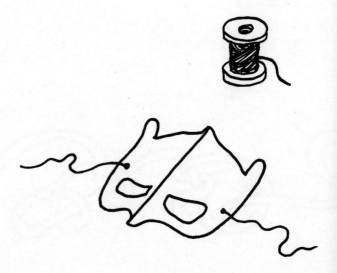

Good night.
You are stunning.
Lay down your burdens.


晚上好。
你魅力四射。
放下你的负担。

Gmorning.

You've had too many apps open for too long.

Close your eyes.

Check all systems.

Soft reboot.


早啊。

你的 app 开得太多太久了。

闭上眼睛。

把系统都检查一遍。

软重启一下吧。

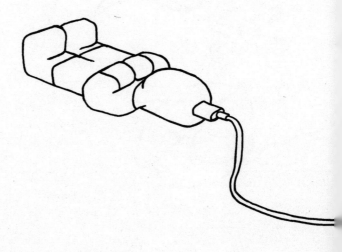

Gnight.

Don't wait until low power mode.

Close your eyes.

Close all unnecessary apps.

Recharge.

晚啊。

别熬到低电量模式再休息。

闭上眼睛。

关掉所有没必要的app。

再去充点电吧。

Good morning!
Rise and shine!
or
Rise and sulk!
or
Rise and weep!
or
Rise and roar!
but
RISE.

早上好！
起来，嗨！
或者
起来，闷！
或者
起来，哭！
或者
起来，吼！
但是
起来吧。

Good night!
Rest and relax!
or
Rest and rejoice!
or
Rest and rejuvenate!
or
Rest and redouble your efforts!
but
REST.

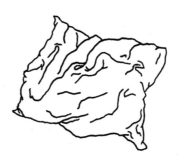

晚上好！
休息，好好放松！
或者
休息，满心喜悦！
或者
休息，恢复青春！
或者
休息，再接再厉！
但是
休息吧。

Good morning.

Keep going.

They will move the goalposts.

They will upend the board when they're in check.

Life WILL be unfair.

YOU keep going.

早上好。

坚持向前。

他们会挪开终点线。

他们会在身处劣势的时候掀桌子。

人生的确会有不公平。

你要坚持向前。

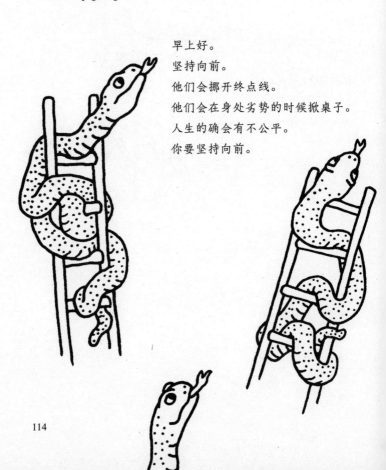

Good night.

Keep going.

They will change the rules on you.

There will be chutes lurking after ladders.

Life's not fair.

YOU keep going.

晚上好。

坚持向前。

他们会对你"双标"。

爬上梯子后，藏着的就是陡坡。

人生就是不公平的。

你要坚持向前。

115

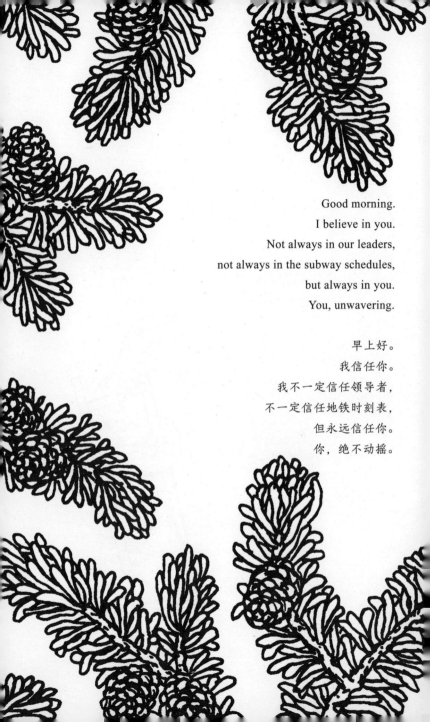

Good morning.
I believe in you.
Not always in our leaders,
not always in the subway schedules,
but always in you.
You, unwavering.

早上好。
我信任你。
我不一定信任领导者,
不一定信任地铁时刻表,
但永远信任你。
你,绝不动摇。

Good night.
I believe in you.
Not always in our institutions,
not always in my own strength,
but always in you.
You, evergreen.

晚上好。
我信任你。
我不一定信任体制，
不一定信任我自己的力量，
但永远信任你。
你，蓊郁常青。

Good morning!

You were lucky enough to wake up today, so cmon.

Socks before shoes, let's go.


早上好！

你真是好运气，还能睁开眼，那就起床吧。

先穿袜子再穿鞋，出发吧。

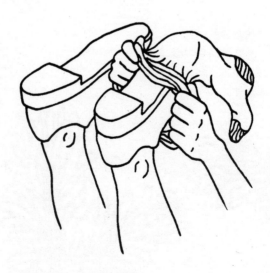

Good night.

You were lucky enough to make it through today, so take it easy.

Brush your teeth, *a dormir*, let's go.

晚上好。

你真是好运气，今天撑过来了，那就放轻松吧。

刷个牙，睡好觉，来吧。

Gmorning!
This first school dance in the gym is hella scary
but good music is playing,
and your friends are here,
so f*** it, let's DANCE.


早啊！
体育馆里的第一次学校舞会还真可怕。
但音乐实在好听，
而朋友都在身边，
去他的，舞起来。

Gnight!
The first school dance in the gym is hella scary,
it's dark in here,
but the music is loud
and we'll never be this young again, let's DANCE.

晚啊!
体育馆里的第一次学校舞会还真可怕,
这儿真够黑的,
但音乐真的好响
青春一去不复回, 舞起来。

Gmorning. Bring it in. Group hug. Okay.
Proceed.

早啊。进来吧。挤成一团抱抱。好了。
走吧。

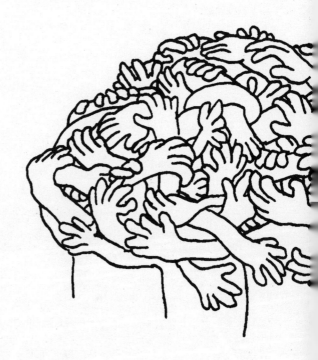

Gnight, guys. One more group hug. *Así.*
Get some sleep.

晚啊，大伙儿。再来抱一团。好了。
睡吧。

Good morning.

You got good head on your shoulders.

As for your shoulders?

F***ing magnificent.

GO get'em today.


早上好。

你肩上那颗脑袋不错。

至于你的肩膀?

堪称奇迹。

今天炸翻全场。

Good night.
Rest your weary head
and those incredible shoulders.
You did good today.

晚上好。
好好休息你的脑瓜
放松那伟岸双肩。
今天干得不错。

Good morning.
Dubious.
But doing this.


早上好。
忐忑踌躇。
却不退缩。

Good night.
Full of doubt.
But singin' out.

晚上好。
满怀疑虑。
道别以歌。

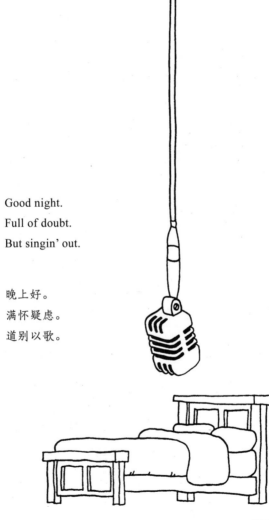

Gmorning.

Your worst fears about yourself only need a drop of attention and sunlight to grow quick and wreck your whole shit.

Clear away those weeds.

Take time to harvest your strengths and your joys.

Water and sunlight to the best in you.

早啊。

心中最大的恐惧只要一点关注和阳光，

就会蔓生肆虐，将你毁灭。

摘除这些杂草。

用心培育心中的力量与快乐。

水和阳光，只给你最好的一面。

Gnight.

Doubts may grow as shadows loom,

when you're alone with your thoughts.

Plant music, art, pics of the ones you love

in the darkest corners.

Harvest the fruits of your daydreams and rest.

Water and sunlight to the best in you.

晚啊。

阴霾之下，疑虑渐生，

独处苦思之下，这只是自然而然。

种下音乐、艺术、你心之所爱

在心中至暗的角落。

收获白日梦结出的果实，好好休息。

水和阳光，只给你最好的一面。

Good morning.

Your very presence is intoxicating.


早上好。

你的存在，令人陶醉。

Good night.

Your very absence is sobering.


晚上好。

没有你在，无奈清醒。

Good morning.

Side kick your fears.

Front kick your distractions.

Boom! You go up a belt!


早上好。

侧踢恐惧。

前踢干扰。

轰！你的段位又升了一带！

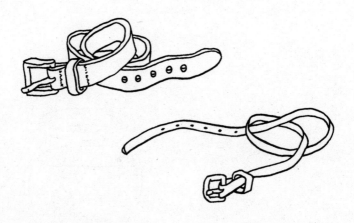

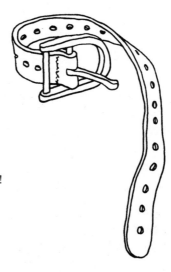

Good night.
Side kick your anxiety.
Front kick your doubts.
Boom! You go up a belt!

晚上好。
侧踢焦虑。
前踢疑惧。
轰！你的段位又升了一带！

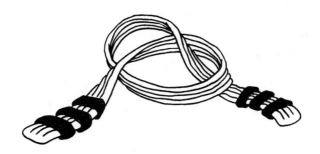

Gmorning.

Look at you!

The miracle of you, the thrill of you

becoming who you'll be!

*spits, wipes your cheek*

Just a little shmutz, got it.

Okay, stunner, GO, they ain't ready for you!


早安。

看看你！

如此的奇迹，如此的激动，

因你将成为你将成为之人！

*沾点口水，擦擦你的脸颊*

只是一点脏，这下搞定了。

好嘞，美人，去吧，他们无法预料到你！

Gnight.

Look at you!

The miracle of you, the thrill of you

becoming who you'll be!

*tousles your hair*

Okay, stunner, REST UP, save some of that perfect for

tomorrow.


晚安。

看看你!

如此的奇迹,如此的激动,

因你将成为你将成为之人!

*揉乱你的头发*

好嘞,美人,休息吧,留一些完美发型给明天。

Gmorning!

No exact recipe for today.

Gather all available ingredients and whip yourself up something delicious.

早安！

今天没有特定的菜谱。

拿出所有的材料，给自己做顿美食。

Gnight.

You whipped up a great day out of all available ingredients!

Feast on the leftovers, reminisce. Enjoy where you've been.

晚安。

你用现有的材料创造了美妙的一天！

享用留下之物，回忆。享受你经历过的地方。

Gmorning!
Use your brains,
use your heart,
use your courage.
And click those heels if you need to peace out!


早安！
用你的大脑，
用你的心，
用你的勇气。
如果需要离开，就磕鞋跟！

Gnight!
*clicks heels three times*


晚安!
*磕三次鞋跟*

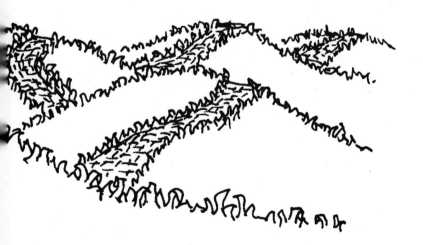

Gmorning.

This feeling will pass.

This workload will pass.

These people will pass.

But look at you, with the gift of memory.

You can time travel to the good stuff just by
closing your eyes & breathing.

Then come right back to now, eyes up for
the good stuff ahead.

You magic thing.


早安。

这情绪会过去。

这工作会过去。

这些人会过去。

但是看看你，你拥有记忆力的馈赠。

只需闭上眼睛，呼吸，

你就可以穿越回那些好事中。

然后再回到现在，准备迎接

未来会有的好事。

你充满魔力。

Gnight.

This moment will pass.

This fatigue will pass.

Tonight will pass.

But look at you, with the gift of imagination.

You can teleport to where you're happiest just by
closing your eyes & breathing.

Then come right back to now, check in with
the present.

You magic thing, you.

晚安。

这一刻会过去。

这疲劳会过去。

这晚上会过去。

但是看看你，你拥有想象力的馈赠。

只需闭上眼睛，呼吸，

你就可以瞬移到最快乐的时光。

然后再回到现在，为现今打卡。

你充满魔力，你啊。

Gmorning from the younger version of you,
who couldn't wait to be you at this age right now.

早安，来自更年轻的你，
他迫不及待成为现在这个年纪的你。

Gnight from the older version of you,
who remembers the very moment you are in right now
and is grinning from ear to ear, because
you have no idea about
the wonders ahead.


晚安，来自更年长的你，
记得你所在的这一刻，
而你正在咧嘴微笑，
因为你根本不知道
未来会有多少美好。

You're indescribable.

We writers spend our lives trying to do you justice.

And you're always more than we can capture.

Good morning.


你无法被描述。

我们这些作家穷尽一生，

试图客观地描绘出你。

而你永远比我们能捕捉到的更多。

早上好。

You're indescribable.
We writers spend our lives trying to
conjure you from every angle.
We get close enough to keep trying.
Good night.


你无法被描述。
我们这些作家穷尽一生，
试图从各个角度变幻出你。
我们也只是将将逼近继续努力的及格线。
晚上好。

Good morning.

Eyes up.

Hearts up.

Minds sharp.

Compassion on full blast.

*sips coffee*

Okay, let's go.


早上好。

直视前方。

内心雀跃。

思想敏锐。

同情心全开。

*呷一口咖啡*

好嘞，出发吧。

Good night.

Eyes shut.

Hearts open.

Minds calm.

Empathy on full blast.

*sips tea*

Okay, let's go.


晚上好。

合上眼睛。

敞开内心。

思想安宁。

同理心全开。

*呷一口茶*

好嘞，睡觉吧。

Gmorning.

Sometimes there are garbage trucks

blocking every road.

They're doing their job and so are you.

Peace to the garbage trucks and the folks

just doing their jobs,

peace to a world that sometimes

puts us at cross purposes,

and peace to you, on your way,

for as long as it takes.


早安。

有的时候垃圾车

会堵住每一条路。

它们只是在做自己的工作，你也一样。

祝愿那些只是在做自己工作的

垃圾车和人们安宁，

祝愿世界安宁，哪怕它偶尔会

让我们有所冲突，

也祝愿正在路上的你安宁，

无论会有多久。

Gnight.

Sometimes there's traffic in every lane,

a galaxy of folks moving in the same direction.

Peace to the kids asleep in backseats,

peace to the miracles of merging lanes, wherein we

inch forward and learn to let each other in,

and peace and patience to you, on your way home.

晚安，

有的时候每个车道都堵车，

一整个星系的人们都往同一个方向去。

祝愿在后座入睡的孩子们安宁，

祝愿并道这一奇迹安宁，它让我们

缓慢前行，并且学会接纳彼此，

祝愿你安宁而耐心，在这回家的路上。

Awaken ancient forms and play within them,
Sift gold amidst the wreckage of your slumber;
Renew your passions, maybe Pinterest pin them,
Tell that one toxic friend, "Yo, lose my number."
The day is clear, new year is aborning;
And so are you, perpet'ually. Gmorning.

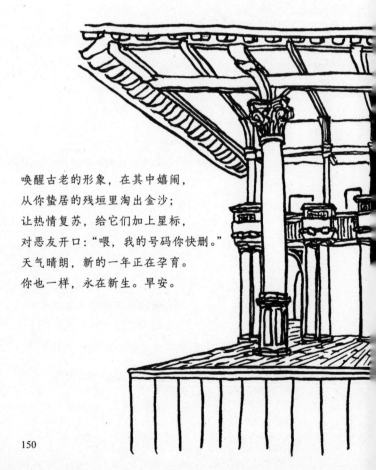

唤醒古老的形象，在其中嬉闹，
从你蛰居的残垣里淘出金沙；
让热情复苏，给它们加上星标，
对恶友开口："喂，我的号码你快删。"
天气晴朗，新的一年正在孕育。
你也一样，永在新生。早安。

Find words for all your daily joys & terrors.
Gnight; make work that gets us in our feelings.
Send off to bed your doubt, your shame, your errors;
Break curfew with muses, shatter ceilings.
The year is fresh; wipe clean inertia's mildew.
Grateful for all you do, & all you will do.

把生活里的快乐与恐惧加以描述。
晚安，着手工作，
给自己的感情找个着落。
上床休息吧，
我们的疑虑、耻辱与错误；
与你的缪斯同闯宵禁，将天花板打破。
新年来临，擦去惰性的绿霉。
对已有的成就，
将来的尝试，心怀感激。

Gmorning!
Yikes, I almost attempted the gmorning
without coffee and a shower.
Take CARE of yourself before leaping into
the world. Take CARE! Love you!

早啊！
哎呀，我说这声早安前
差点没喝咖啡，没冲澡。
好好照顾自己，然后再闯进世界。
照顾自己！爱你！

HHRRRRRRRRRRAHHHHHH

Gnight!
Almost went to bed while reading the news.
Give yourself a minute before you fall asleep;
get your mind right! Love you!

H GAAAAAHHHHHHHHH

晚啊!
看着新闻,差点睡着。
入梦以前,先给自己一刻喘息。
把状态调好! 爱你!

Good morning.

Don't wait on anyone to make your favorite thing.

Make your own favorite thing.

Go.


早上好。

别等着别人创造你的最爱。

最爱要自己去造。

去吧。

Good night.

Don't let anyone set parameters on your dreams.

Your dreams are yours

and yours alone.

Go.


晚上好。

别让任何人为你的梦想设限。

梦想是你的，

只属于你自己。

去吧。

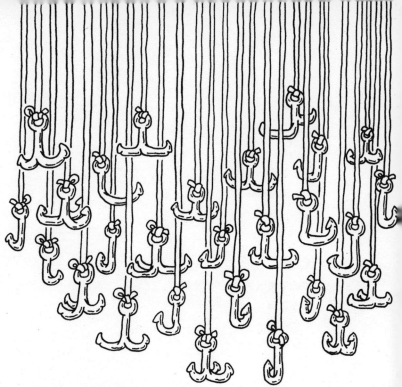

Good morning.

Do NOT get stuck in the comments section of life today.

Make, do, create the things.

Let others tussle it out.

*Vamos*!

早上好。

别把今天纠结在人生的评论区。

制造，行动，创造事物。

让别人打嘴仗去吧。

走吧！

Good night.

Don't let the world's clickbait pull you off your path.

Unplug, explore, dream new terrain.

The world keeps spinning.

*A dormir*!


晚上好。

别让生活的标题党带歪了道路。

拔电，探索，想象全新的领域。

世界照常运行。

睡吧！

Good morning, you.

Yes, you.

YOU RIGHT THERE, LOOKIN' CUTE AS YOU
WANNA BE.

Damn, you gon' knock 'em out today! Go!

早上好啊，你。

对，你。

就是你，看起来真可爱

正如你所愿。

天，你今天要杀翻全场！去吧！

Good night, you.

Yes, you.

You there, LOOKIN' FRESH AS HELL.

Check you out.

Leavin' a trail of people dreaming about you in your wake.


晚上好啊，你。

对，你。

就是你，爽利得无与伦比。

好好看看你。

一觉醒来

留下那么一大串人对你魂牵梦萦。

Gmorning.

Unclench your fists.

Lower your shoulders.

Step away.

Then come back with a clear head,

redouble your efforts.

I believe in you.


早安。

松开拳头。

放松肩膀。

走开吧。

清醒了再回来，

加倍努力。

我对你有信心。

Gnight.
Unclench your fists.
Lower your shoulders.
Step away.
Come back with a clear head mañana,
redouble your efforts.
I believe in you.

晚安。
松开拳头。
放松肩膀。
走开吧。
明天清醒了再来一遍,
加倍努力。
我对你有信心。

Good morning.
I know it seems like everyone left
without you for the party,
and those stepsisters suck,
but us woodland creatures are on your side.


早上好。
我懂，所有人好像都去派对了，
就不带你去，
继姐妹也糟透顶，
但我们森林生灵都与你同在。

Good night.

I know it seems like everyone is at the Prince's ball
all the time,

but it's okay to go home before midnight.

Kick off your shoes.


晚上好。

我懂，所有人都好像在王子的舞会

成天作乐，

但半夜以前回家也没问题。

脚上那双鞋踢掉吧。

Good morning.
If we're picking teams,
I call dibs on you.
Thanks for being around.

早上好。
如果要选一队，
我押你一定赢。
感谢有你在。

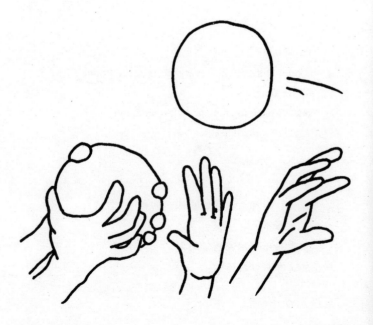

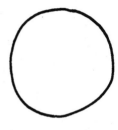

Good night.
Great team, great game.
You are CLUTCH!

晚上好。
好队伍，好比赛。
你真绝了！

Good morning, people of every color, shape, and stripe! Hold up: you with the stripes, get over here, that's awesome!

早上好，无论你什么肤色、体型，或是花纹！
站住，有条纹的那个，
你过来，真太好了！

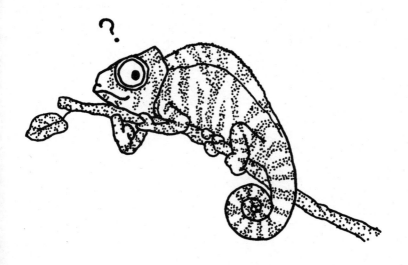

Good night, people of every shape, color, and stripe.
And those of you who change colors in the sun.


晚上好，无论你什么肤色、体型，或是花纹。
还有阳光下会变色的你们。

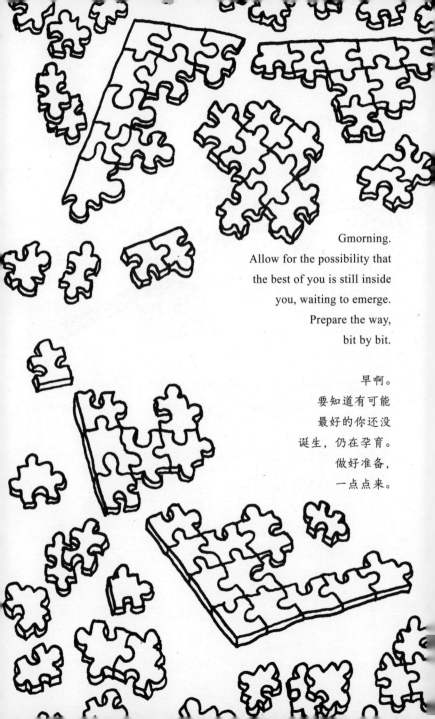

Gmorning.
Allow for the possibility that
the best of you is still inside
you, waiting to emerge.
Prepare the way,
bit by bit.

早啊。
要知道有可能
最好的你还没
诞生，仍在孕育。
做好准备，
一点点来。

Gnight.
Allow for the possibility that
the best stuff is still ahead of
you, waiting to reveal itself.
Prepare the way,
bit by bit.

晚啊。
要知道有可能
最好的事物仍在前方，
等着亮相。
做好准备，
一点点来。

Good morning!

You are the bees' knees!

The lambs' gams!

The calves' calves!

Bethenny Frankel's ankles!

Invent new idioms!

Let's go!

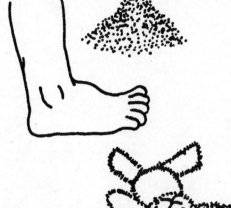

早上好！

你是蜜蜂的风！

羊羔的膏！

牛仔的仔！

贝辛妮·弗兰凯的脚踝！

来造点新词！

走吧！

Good night!
You're the cream in my coffee!
The sugar in my bowl!
The absinthe in my cocktail!
The syrup in my Slurpee!
Tasty dreams, let's go!

晚上好！
你是我咖啡里的奶油！
碗里的白糖！
鸡尾酒里的苦艾！
冰沙里的糖浆！
美味好梦，我们来了！

Good morning.
Words fail us, often, but when we put 'em together the
right way they can pull boulders out of us.
Keep working with 'em.

早上好。
语言不能尽述，
但只要措辞方式得当，
就能吐出胸中块垒。
好好运用。

Good night.

Tomorrow we take pen to pad, move mountains.

Get some rest.


晚上好。

明天我们执笔落字，以此搬山。

休息一下。

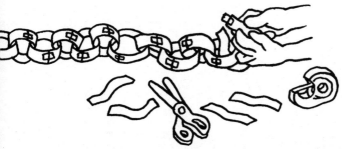

Good morning.

It's okay to let your mind drift.

Whoa, cool drift, kid!


早上好。

走神也没关系。

嚯，走位风骚啊，小子！

Good night.

So glad we're drift compatible.

晚上好。

真高兴咱们走位很搭。

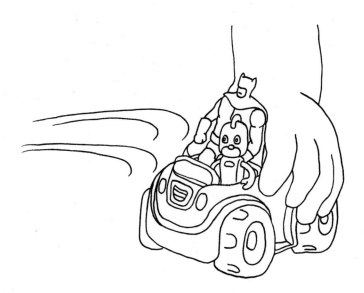

Gmorning.

You're stunning and the world is

lucky to have you.

We are LUCKY TO HAVE YOU.

Do your best.


早安。

你如此迷人，

世界能够拥有你实属幸运。

我们能拥有你实属幸运。

尽你所能。


Gnight.

You're stunning and the world is

lucky to have you.

We are LUCKY TO HAVE YOU.

Get some rest.

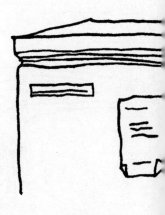

晚安。

你如此迷人，

世界能够拥有你实属幸运。

我们能拥有你实属幸运。

好好休息。

Good morning.

Give a little more than you think you can today.

It'll come back around somehow, I promise.

That's what I got for you.

早上好。

在今天，稍稍超越自己。

未来会以某种方式回报你，我保证。

这是我给你的承诺。

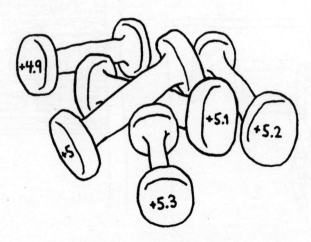

Good night.

New ideas are waiting for you on

the other side of sleep.

Don't be afraid of going to meet 'em.

Yeah? Yeah.


晚上好。

新的主意在等着你

就在入睡的那一侧。

大胆去和它们邂逅。

是吧？嗯。

Gmorning.

Subways may be slow.

Traffic may crawl to a halt.

Still, you're on your way.

You are not defined by the speed of your surroundings.

Your mind is racing.

You're on your way, damnit.

早安。

地铁或许进度缓慢。

交通或许龟速停滞。

不过，你仍然在路上。

你并非由周围事物的
速度而定义。

你的思想风驰电掣。

你就在路上，真倒霉。

Gnight.

Days may be slow.

You may face setbacks.

Still, you're on your way.

Your tempo is not dictated by your surroundings.

Your heartbeat is your own.

You're on your way, damnit.

晚安。

白天或许进度缓慢。

你或许面临挫折。

不过，你仍然在路上。

你的节奏并非由周围事物而定义。

你的心跳只属于你。

你就在路上，真倒霉。

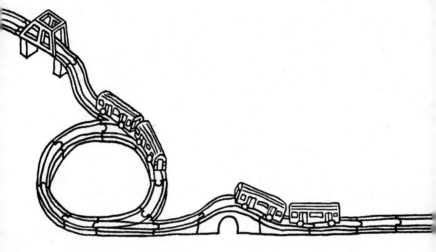

Gmorning.
Try and face the world with
your best self, even if the world
doesn't respond in kind.
Don't do them, do you.

早安。
试着以最好的自己面对世界，
即使世界并不相应回报。
别做他们，做你。

Gnight.

Tomorrow we try again.

Rest up.


晚安。

明天我们再次尝试。

好好休息。

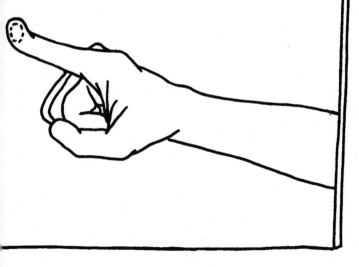

Good morning.

Courage.

Even when the panic's at the back of your throat,

courage.

Let's go.


早上好。

勇敢起来。

即使惊慌躲在你的喉咙口，

勇敢起来。

上吧。

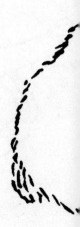

Good night.

Courage.

Even when fear is at the foot of your bed, courage.

Let's go.


晚安。

勇敢起来。

即使恐惧在你的床脚，勇敢起来。

上吧。

Gmorning.

Set the thermostat for your heart today.

The temp where you like it.

You know yourself, you know what you need.

Take your time.

早安。

在今天，给你的心定好调温器。

定你喜欢的温度。

你了解自己，你了解自己的需要。

别急。

Gnight.

Set the thermostat for your heart tonight.

The temp where you like it.

You know yourself, you know what you need.

Take your time.

晚安。

在今晚，给你的心定好调温器。

定你喜欢的温度。

你了解自己，你了解自己的需要。

别急。

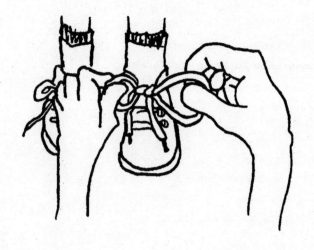

Good morning.
Take care of each other.
Take care of yourself.
Repeat.


早上好。
照顾好彼此。
照顾好自己。
重复。

Good night.

Take care of each other.

Take care of yourself.

Repeat.


晚上好。

照顾好彼此。

照顾好自己。

重复。

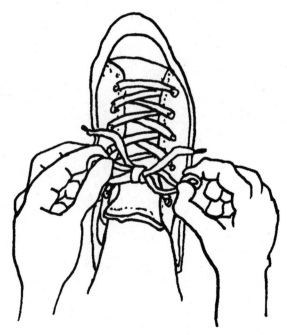

Gmorning.

Look at you!

Damn, you all right!

Pssh. They ain't ready for you!

早安。

看看你！

哎哟，你真的很不错！

嘘，打他们个措手不及！

Gnight.

Dag, check you out!

Told you they weren't ready.

Rest all that greatness!


晚安。

哎呀，瞅瞅你!

都说了他们会措手不及。

伟大的你，好好休息吧!

Good morning.
You will have to say no to things to say yes
to your work.
It will be worth it.


早上好。
为了对工作说是，你会对有些事说不。
它会是值得的。

Good night.

Don't forget to look up from your work &

let real life in.

It makes your work better.

晚上好。

别忘了从工作中抬起头，让真正的生活进来。

它会让你的工作更好。

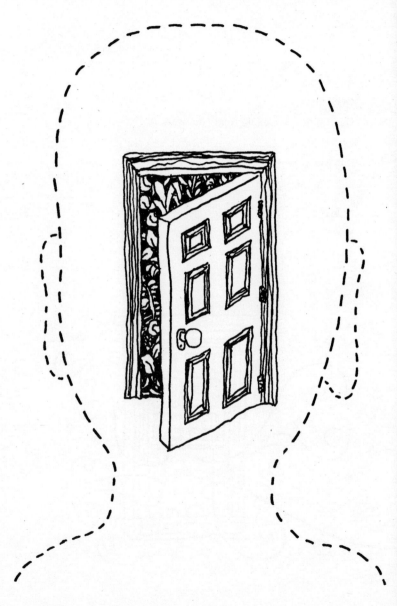

Gmorning.

Get out of your own head for a sec.

Do something good today for someone else.

They'll appreciate it

(and so will your head).


早安。

跳出思想一秒钟。

为别人做件好事。

他们会很感激

（你的思想也会）。


Gnight.

Climb back into your own head for a sec.

Take stock of what you've got, and what

you need.

You'll appreciate it

(and so will your head).


晚安。

钻回思想一秒钟。

盘点你已有的东西和你需要的东西。

你会很感激

（你的思想也会）。

Good morning.

You are perfectly cast in your life.

I can't imagine anyone but you in the role.

Go play.


早上好。

你是你这一生完美的选角。

我无法想象他人扮演这个角色，除了你。

准备上场啦。

Good night.

You are perfectly cast in your life.

And with so little rehearsal too!

It's a joy to watch. Thank you.

晚上好。

你是你这一生完美的选角。

而且甚至没有怎么彩排！

看起来如此令人愉悦。谢谢你。

Gmorning.

Pain, joy, frustration, euphoria, everything.

It all passes. It all keeps moving.

Wherever you are is temporary.

Let's go!


早安。

痛苦、喜悦、挫败、欣快，所有的一切。

都会过去，都会继续向前。

无论你在哪里，都是暂时的。

走吧！

Gnight.

Rage, bliss, fatigue, rapture, everything.

It all passes. It all keeps moving.

Where you are is fleeting.

*Andiamo*.


晚安。

愤怒、极乐、疲劳、狂喜，所有的一切。

都会过去。都会继续向前。

你所在之地稍纵即逝。

开始了。

Gmorning.

Tired, but grateful.

Sick, but grateful.

It's grey out, but I'm grateful.

So much easier to start with grateful.


早安。

疲惫，但是感恩。

厌烦，但是感恩。

外面晦暗不明，但是我感恩。

由感恩开始会容易得多。

Gnight.

Tired, but grateful.

Sick, but grateful.

It's dark out, but I'm grateful.

So much easier to end with grateful.

晚安。

疲惫，但是感恩。

厌烦，但是感恩。

外面夜暮蔼蔼，但是我感恩。

由感恩结束会容易得多。

# 致 谢

　　林-曼纽尔和乔尼想让你知道，如果没有那些在推特上与我们交谈的人（我们深情地称之为Twitterico），本书不可能诞生。我们也要感谢卡珊德拉·特灵、本·格林伯格（Ben Greenberg）。感谢WME公司的约翰·巴泽蒂（John Buzzetti）、安迪·麦克尼科尔（Andy McNicol），LGR Literary公司的丹尼尔·格林伯格（Daniel Greenberg）、蒂姆·沃伊奇克（Tim Wojcik）。感谢设计师西蒙·沙利文（Simon Sullivan）、短信群里的莎拉·凯（Sarah Kay）。感谢《龙猫》（*My Neighbor Totoro*），还有《龙猫》里的爸爸。感谢瓦妮莎·纳达尔（Vanessa Nadal）、艾丽莎·卡卡维拉（Elissa Caccavella）。感谢塞巴斯蒂安·米兰达（Sebastian Miranda）、弗朗西斯科·米兰达（Francisco Miranda）和托比洛·米兰达（Tobillo Miranda）。感谢克里斯托弗·孙（Christopher Sun）。感谢孙一家和卡卡维拉一家。还有每天将早晨与夜晚带给我们的太阳。

**图书在版编目（CIP）数据**

早安，晚安 / (波多)林-曼纽尔·米兰达著；(加)
乔尼·孙绘；符夏怡，雷亚兰译. -- 北京：中国友谊
出版公司，2021.11
书名原文：Gmorning, Gnight!: Little Pep Talks
for Me & You
ISBN 978-7-5057-5324-2

Ⅰ.①早… Ⅱ.①林… ②乔… ③符… ④雷… Ⅲ.
①诗集－波多黎各－现代 Ⅳ.① I755.25

中国版本图书馆 CIP 数据核字 (2021) 第 190515 号

**著作权合同登记号 图字：01-2021-5991**

| | |
|---|---|
| 书名 | 早安，晚安 |
| 作者 | ［波多黎各］林-曼纽尔·米兰达 |
| 绘者 | ［加拿大］乔尼·孙 |
| 译者 | 符夏怡　雷亚兰 |
| 出版 | 中国友谊出版公司 |
| 发行 | 中国友谊出版公司 |
| 经销 | 新华书店 |
| 印刷 | 鸿博昊天科技有限公司 |
| 规格 | 787×1092 毫米 32 开 |
| | 6.75 印张　60 千字 |
| 版次 | 2022 年 2 月第 1 版 |
| 印次 | 2022 年 2 月第 1 次印刷 |
| 书号 | ISBN 978-7-5057-5324-2 |
| 定价 | 68.00 元 |
| 地址 | 北京市朝阳区西坝河南里 17 号楼 |
| 邮编 | 100028 |
| 电话 | （010）64678009 |